You're Not My REAL Mother!

by **Molly Friedrich**

Illustrated by **Christy Hale**

LITTLE, BROWN AND COMPANY

New York ✦ Boston

Little, Brown and Company

Time Warner Book Group
1271 Avenue of the Americas, New York, NY 10020
Visit our Web site at www.lb-kids.com

First Edition

Library of Congress Cataloging-in-Publication Data

Friedrich, Molly.
You're not my real mother! / by Molly Friedrich ; illustrated by Christy Hale. — 1st ed.
p. cm.
Summary: After an adoptive mother tells her daughter all the reasons that she is her "real mother,"
the young girl realizes that her mother is right, even though they do not look alike.
ISBN 0-316-60553-0
[1. Adoption — Fiction. 2. Mothers — Fiction. 3. Self-perception — Fiction. 4. Identity — Fiction.]
I. Title: You're not my real mother!. II. Hale, Christy, ill. III. Title.
PZ7.F91515Yo 2004
[E] — dc22   2003054574

10   9   8   7   6   5   4   3   2   1

SC

Manufactured in China

The illustrations for this book were done in mixed media
on Arches Cold Pressed Watercolor paper.
The text was set in Providence Sans and Futura Book, and
the display type is Providence Sans Bold.

To Julia, Lucy, P-Quy, and Fernando,
with much love from their REAL mother
—M.F.

For Carolyn Rubenstein
—C.H.

What do you mean, my darling?
Of course I'm your real mother!

Does a real mother let you put twenty bandages
on a bruised knee when you really only need one?

The more, the better!

And does a real mother drive to Parker's house to pick up Polar Bear when you've left him there?

He would have been so lonely without me!

Does a real mother help you cook stew by peeling carrots, cutting green beans, and rolling the beef cubes in flour?

Yes, and Shelly helps too!

Does a real mother teach you to say "please" and "thank you" and "I had a very nice time"?

And, "If you want to be my friend, don't push me!"

Does a real mother teach you the alphabet and how to count to a hundred by tens?

Ten, twenty, thirty, forty...

Does a real mother teach you how to tie your shoes? Zip up your jacket? Brush your teeth . . . even the way-back molars?

And does a real mother
love you, hug you,
smother you with kisses,
and try to gobble you up
because you are so irresistible?

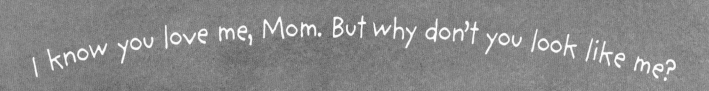

I don't look like you because
I'm not your birth mother.

Who's that?

Your birth mother is the mother who gave birth to you. She started your life, and I am thankful to her every day for that.

Why?

Because I get to watch you grow!

You let me hold
Shelly's leash!

At least part of the way, until
she spots a rushing squirrel.

You show me how to do a perfect cannonball to make the biggest splash!

Like a tidal wave!

You jump with me on the trampoline!

Higher than the forsythia!

You help me catch fireflies
way after bedtime.

Sometimes it's okay to
break the rules, right?

You sing songs halfway through and
fall asleep before me and Polar Bear.

Hmmm? What? I do?

Yes, you do, and
do you know why?

Because you're my
bandage-putting, car-driving,
beef stew–cooking,
please-and-thank-you–teaching,
alphabet-saying, tens-counting,
shoe-tying, jacket-zipping, teeth-brushing,
kiss-smothering,
cannonball-splashing,
trampoline-jumping,
firefly-catching,
halfway-song–singing
REAL MOTHER!